FRIENDS
OF ACPL

TRICERATOPS

THE LAST DINOSAUR

by

Elizabeth J. Sandell

DINOSAUR DISCOVERY ERA

Bancroft-Sage Publishing
112 Marshall St., Box 1968, Mankato, MN 56001-1968 USA

LIBRARY OF CONGRESS CATALOGING IN PUBLICATION DATA

Sandell, Elizabeth J.
  Triceratops: the last dinosaur.

  (Dinosaur discovery era)
  SUMMARY: Presents presently-known information on the plant-eating dinosaur that looked like a rhinoceros.
  1. Triceratops--Juvenile literature. (1. Triceratops. 2. Dinosaurs.) I. Oelerich, Marjorie L. II. Schroeder, Howard. III. Vista III Design. IV. Title. V. Series.
  QE862.065S36   1988   567.9'7   88-952
  ISBN 0-944280-01-3 (lib. bdg.)
  ISBN 0-944280-07-2 (pbk. bdg.)

International Standard **Book Number:** Library Binding 0-944280-01-3 Paperback Binding 0-944280-07-2	**Library of Congress** **Catalog Card Number:** 88-952

SPECIAL THANKS FOR THEIR HELP AND COOPERATION TO:
Mary R. Carman, Paleontology Collection Manager
Field Museum of Natural History
Chicago, Illinois

TRICERATOPS

THE LAST DINOSAUR

AUTHOR

Elizabeth J. Sandell

dedicated with love to Denny

EDITED BY

Marjorie L. Oelerich, Ph.D.
Professor of Early Childhood and Elementary Education
Mankato State University

Howard Schroeder, Ph.D.
Professor of Reading and Language Arts
Dept. of Curriculum and Instruction
Mankato State University
Mankato, MN

ILLUSTRATED BY

Vista III Design

BANCROFT-SAGE PUBLISHING

112 Marshall St., Box 1968, Mankato, MN 56001-1968 U.S.A.

INTRODUCTION: GARR FINDS FOSSILS

Sometimes when Garr goes walking in the country, he finds different kinds of rocks. His favorites are called fossils.

The best fossil Garr ever found looked like a footprint from a big animal. It was about 24 inches (61 cm) long. Next to it was another fossil which looked like an egg. Garr took both fossils to school to show his teacher and classmates.

Garr's teacher, Mr. Finley, looked at the two fossils.

"These do look like a footprint and an egg," he said. "They could be from a dinosaur.

"May I take your fossils and show them to my friend, Dr. Sanford?" Mr. Finley continued. "She knows all about fossils. She is a special scientist called a paleontologist. Dr. Sanford studies fossils to learn about animals and plants that lived many years ago."

Garr wanted to know more about fossils. So, he let Mr. Finley take them.

The next week, Mr. Finley told Garr and the class what he had learned from Dr. Sanford.

"The footprint and egg might have been left by a dinosaur called *Triceratops*," Mr. Finley said. "These animals lived on parts of the earth for many years. Of all the kinds of dinosaurs, *Triceratops* was one of the last. Scientists are not sure why this is so. Maybe it was because *Triceratops* was one of the last dinosaurs to appear."

The class wanted to learn more about *Triceratops*. Garr and the other students had many questions about this dinosaur.

"Garr, you found the fossils. What would you like to learn about *Triceratops*?" Mr. Finley asked.

Garr answered, "I want to know what *Triceratops* looked like. I want to know how smart it was."

"I want to know about *Triceratops'* family. And I wonder how that dinosaur would fight!" exclaimed Ryan.

Rosa said, "I would like to find out why there are no *Triceratops* alive today."

The class began their study. They read many books. They looked at a number of pictures. At the end, they had a Dinosaur News Report. They told each other what they had learned about *Triceratops*.

CHAPTER 1: TRICERATOPS LOOKED LIKE A RHINOCEROS

Triceratops (tri ser´ uh tops´) looked like a rhinoceros (ri nos´ uhr uhs). But it was about twice as long. And it weighed more than a rhinoceros.

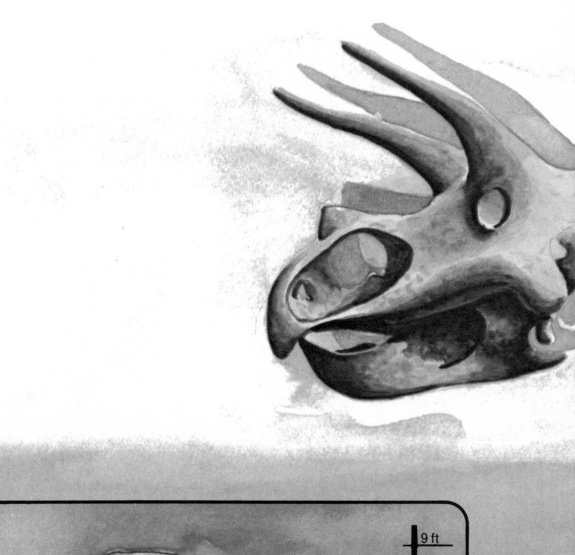

LENGTH, HEIGHT, AND WEIGHT

Triceratops was 25 to 30 feet (8 to 10 m) long from the tip of its nose to the end of its tail. When standing, it was 8 to 9 feet (2.4 to 2.8 m) tall. The skull of its head was nearly 7 feet (2.1 m) from the nose to the edge of its neck frill. It weighed 5 to 6 tons (4.5 to 5.4 metric tons), which is almost as much as a big elephant.

Triceratops was one of the largest animals that ever lived. Some scientists believe that dinosaurs kept growing as long as they lived. This would help to explain the fact that dinosaurs became so big.

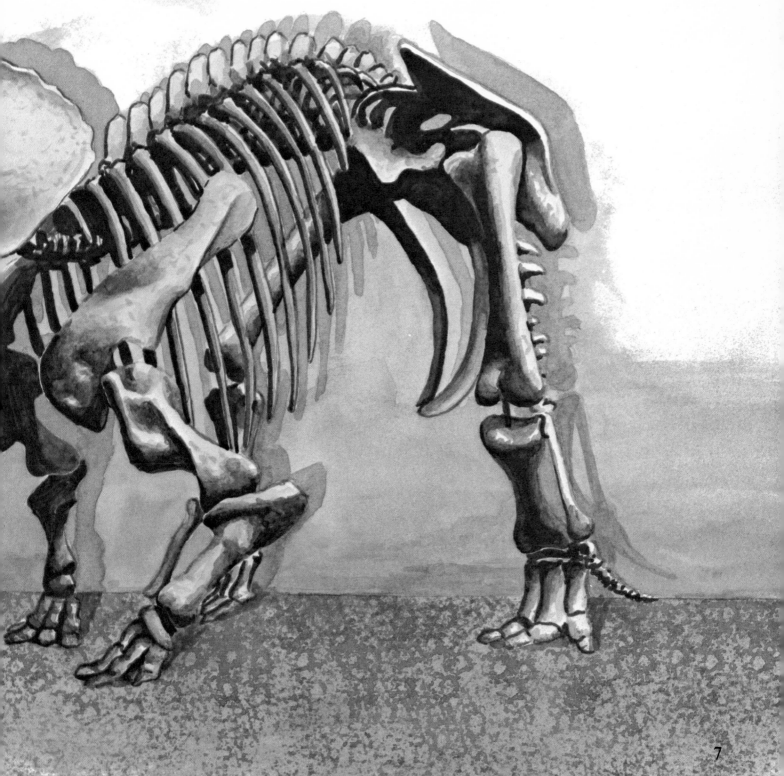

THREE-HORNED FACE

The word *Triceratops* means "three-horned face." It comes from two Greek words. The Greek word **tri** for "three" was put with the Greek word **keratops** for "horned face." There was one thick, strong horn on its nose. And there was a horn above each eye. Each of these two horns was about 40 inches (1 m) long.

The very big jaws did not have teeth in the front. There was a row of teeth in the back of each jaw. The lower teeth closed inside the upper teeth. Fossils have been found which show that the teeth were worn smooth. Scientists believe these teeth dropped out of the dinosaur's mouth. Then the dinosaur might have grown new teeth.

PROTECTED BY A FRILLED SHIELD AND THICK SKIN

One of the most unusual features of *Triceratops* was its frilled shield, which was at the base of its big head. This frill was broad, smooth, and solid. It was called a frill because the edge looked like a ruffle. This shield protected its neck and shoulders. It might also have held up shoulder muscles.

Triceratops had thick skin which was as tough as leather. The skin was so tough that it helped protect *Triceratops* from the claws and teeth of its enemies.

SMELLING, SEEING, AND HEARING

It was important for *Triceratops* to be able to tell when enemies were coming. Through smelling, seeing, and hearing, it could know when it was in danger. Also, to find plants for food, it needed to be able to smell and see them.

Some fossils of *Triceratops* show the kind of head this dinosaur had. The nose was big. It was shaped like the beak of a parrot. Scientists believe that *Triceratops* had a very good sense of smell.

Scientists study the size of the eye spaces in the skull. *Triceratops* had large eye spaces, which means it had large eyes. The skull also shows that the eyes were set far apart. They were at the front of the head. All of this means that *Triceratops* may have had very good eyesight.

Some scientists believe that *Triceratops* could hear very well. This would suggest that it was also able to make sounds. However, fossils do not show what sounds *Triceratops* may have made.

LEGS AND FEET

Triceratops walked on all four feet. It had thick, strong legs. Its back legs were longer than the front legs. On each of the back feet were five toes. One of these toes was very small. Each of the front feet had four toes. Each toe had a claw. Scientists believe it may have been able to run about 30 miles (50 km) per hour.

CHAPTER 2:
TRICERATOPS WAS SMART

Scientists do not really know how smart the dinosaurs were. Scientists used to think that the size of the brain showed how wise the animal was. In that case, *Triceratops* was not very clever, because it had a brain about as small as a walnut.

A newer idea is that we learn about an animal's thinking by how the animal lived. Some scientists believe that the dinosaurs were smarter than we used to suppose. Many of the things dinosaurs did to take care of their young were very wise.

PLANT-EATER

Triceratops ate only plants. Because its teeth were in the back of the jaws, it was not able to chew grass. It would eat leaves and twigs from trees. Maybe it pushed over tall trees to get at the top branches. This dinosaur could have grabbed the tree trunk in its mouth and pulled the tree to the ground.

MATING AND NESTING

A group of *Triceratops* would live together as a family. They would help one another within the group. They would protect each other from enemies.

When it was time to mate, two male *Tricertops* might fight to get females to notice them. The males might bang their heads together, lock the horns on each other, and push very hard. Usually, they did not hurt each other. They just wanted to show the female *Triceratops* which male was stronger.

Fossils of dinosaur nests and eggs have been found. Fossil bones of baby and adult dinosaurs have been found near the nests. The dinosaurs made mud nests on the ground. The eggs were found in circles inside the nests. Scientists believe that after the eggs hatched, the baby dinosaurs grew slowly into adult dinosaurs.

The mother would take care of the young dinosaurs until they could hunt and live on their own. The neck frills and horns probably did not grow to full size until the young dinosaur was quite big. Remember, the frill and horns were needed for protection. The dinosaur could not protect itself until these parts were strong.

Scientists know from fossil footprints that the young dinosaurs were kept in the middle of the herd as the dinosaurs walked. The fully-grown dinosaurs would walk on the outside to be ready for enemies.

FIGHTING ENEMIES

Triceratops was stronger than most of its enemies because of its horns and frill. As long as it kept its enemy in front, *Triceratops* was safe.

Scientists believe that it used its horns like spears for attacking others and for defending itself. When it attacked, *Triceratops* could point its horns at the enemy and lower its head. It could push the horns into the softest part of the enemy.

Like some animals today, *Triceratops* might fight for four reasons: 1) protect itself from enemies, 2) defend its territory, 3) win a mate, and 4) become the leader of the herd.

CHAPTER 3:
THE WORLD OF TRICERATOPS

Thousands of years ago, the land on earth may have moved slowly apart.

Earthquakes and volcanoes caused the land to shake and move in many different directions. In the western part of North America, earthquakes caused the Rocky Mountains to be formed.

During this time, scientists believe that the land looked like this map.

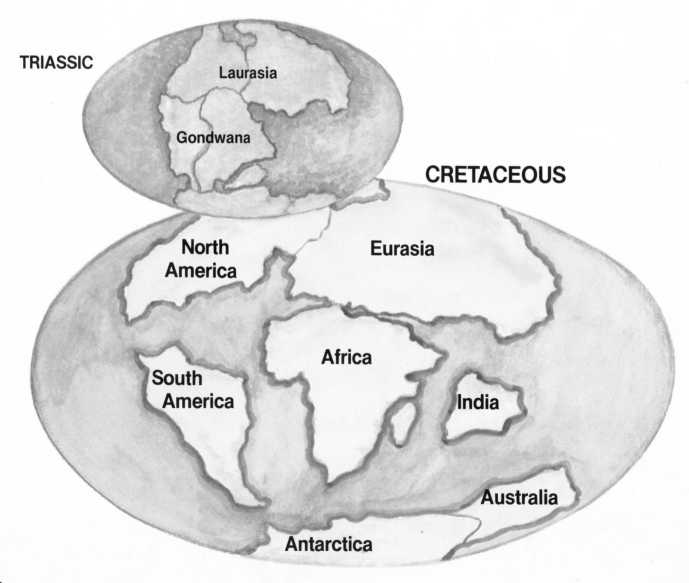

WHERE TRICERATOPS LIVED

The weather was warm and pleasant when *Triceratops* lived.

A sea covered the area from the Arctic to Canada, and down to Minnesota, Arkansas, and New Mexico.

Ferns, grasses, and many plants grew near this sea. There were many kinds of trees, such as palm, willow, walnut, and oak. Some trees grew as tall as 40 to 50 feet (12 to 15 m).

Triceratops lived in the western part of North America. Skeletons have been found in Montana, Wyoming, and Colorado (USA), and in Alberta and Saskatchewan (Canada).

CHAPTER 4:
TRICERATOPS DISAPPEARED

Many dinosaurs lived to a very old age. From fossils, scientists know that some dinosaurs lived to be 200 years old. Bones show that many dinosaurs lived at least 120 years.

REASONS DINOSAURS DIED

Why did all the dinosaurs die? Scientists are not sure. Some scientists think the earth became cold. Others think the earth flooded with water. Maybe a star exploded in space and caused energy rays to kill the dinosaurs. Or a rock might have crashed into earth. This could then have made clouds of dust that blocked out the sunlight.

FOSSILS FORMED

When the dinosaurs died, the bodies of some were covered with sand and mud. Some bones of these dinosaurs turned into fossils. Many years later, the fossils of *Triceratops,* with the three-horned face, were found.

CONCLUSION: QUESTIONS ABOUT TRICERATOPS

Although some things are known about *Triceratops,* there is much to learn.

For example, paleontologists (pa´ le on tol´ uh jists) really don't know exactly what *Triceratops* looked like.

Scientists don't know how smart dinosaurs were.

Also, no one knows why all of them died.

Scientists will keep looking. Maybe someday they will find some more answers.

MUSEUMS

Fossil skeletons, plaster casts, and fiberglass casts of *Triceratops* may be seen in several museums. You may want to visit them.

American Museum of Natural History, New York, NY.

Buffalo Museum of Science, Buffalo, NY.

Field Museum of Natural History, Chicago, IL.

National Museum of Natural History, Smithsonian Institution, Washington, DC.

National Museum of Natural Sciences, Ottawa, Ontario (Canada).

Peabody Museum of Natural History, Yale University, New Haven, CT.

Science Museum of Minnesota, St. Paul, MN.

Tyrrell Museum of Paleontology, Drumheller, Alberta (Canada).

Zoological Gardens, Calgary, Alberta (Canada).

GLOSSARY

DINOSAUR (di´ nuh sor´) means "terrible lizard." The Greek word **deinos** means "terrible," and the word **sauros** means "lizard."

FOSSILS (fos´ uhlz) are the remains of plants and animals that lived many years ago. The Latin word **fossilis** means "something dug up."

FRILL (fril) is the ruffled, hard shield at the base of the head of Triceratops.

MUSEUM (myoo ze´ uhm) is a place for keeping and exhibiting works of nature and art, scientific objects, and other items.

PALEONTOLOGIST (pa´ le on tol´ uh jist) is a person who studies fossils to learn about plants and animals from thousands of years ago. The Greek word **palaios** means "ancient," **onta** means "living things," and **logos** means "talking about."

RHINOCEROS (ri nos´ uhr uhs) is a large, plant-eating mammal of Africa and Asia which has one or two horns on its snout and a very thick hide.

SCIENTIST (si´ uhn tist) is a person who studies objects or events.

SKELETON (skel´ uh tuhn) is the framework of bones of a body.

SKULL (skul) is the bony framework of the head of an animal.

THOUSAND (thou´ zuhnd) is ten times one hundred. It is shown as 1,000.

TRICERATOPS (tri ser´ uh tops´) was a large plant-eating dinosaur that had a horn above each eye and one horn above the nose. The name means three-horned face from the Greek words **tri** "for three" and **keratops** "for horned face."

TIME LINE

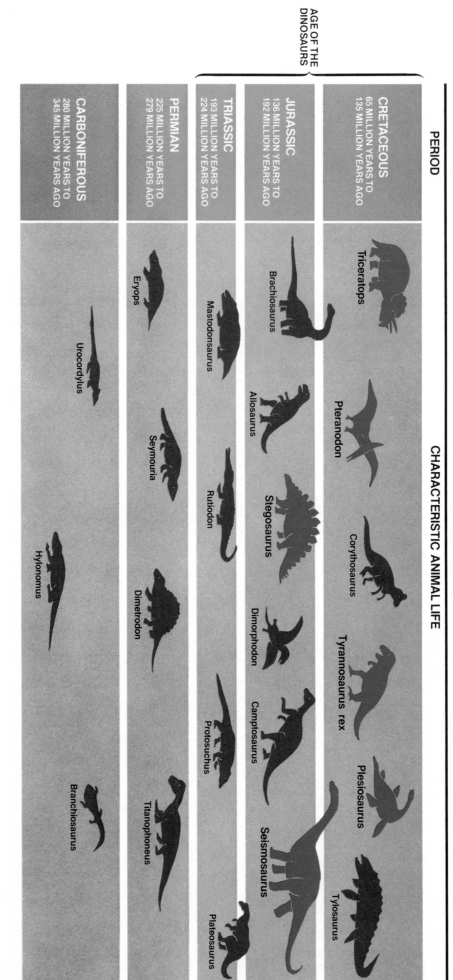

PERIOD

CHARACTERISTIC ANIMAL LIFE

AGE OF THE DINOSAURS

CRETACEOUS
65 MILLION YEARS TO
135 MILLION YEARS AGO

Triceratops · Pteranodon · Corythosaurus · Tyrannosaurus rex · Plesiosaurus · Tylosaurus

JURASSIC
136 MILLION YEARS TO
192 MILLION YEARS AGO

Brachiosaurus · Allosaurus · Stegosaurus · Dimorphodon · Camptosaurus · Seismosaurus

TRIASSIC
193 MILLION YEARS TO
224 MILLION YEARS AGO

Mastodonsaurus · Rutiodon · Protosuchus · Plateosaurus

PERMIAN
225 MILLION YEARS TO
279 MILLION YEARS AGO

Eryops · Seymouria · Dimetrodon · Titanophoneus

CARBONIFEROUS
280 MILLION YEARS TO
345 MILLION YEARS AGO

Urocordylus · Hylonomus · Branchiosaurus